Dear Parents,

Welcome to the Scholastic Reader series. We have taken over 80 years of experience with teachers, parents, and children and put it into a program that is designed to match your child's interests and skills.

Level 1—Short sentences and stories made up of words kids can sound out using their phonics skills and words that are important to remember.

Level 2—Longer sentences and stories with words kids need to know and new "big" words that they will want to know.

Level 3—From sentences to paragraphs to longer stories, these books have large "chunks" of text and are made up of a rich vocabulary.

Level 4—First chapter books with more words and fewer pictures.

It is important that children learn to read well enough to succeed in school and beyond. Here are ideas for reading this book with your child:

- Look at the book together. Encourage your child to read the title and make a prediction about the story.
- Read the book together. Encourage your child to sound out words when appropriate. When your child struggles, you can help by providing the word.
- Encourage your child to retell the story. This is a great way to check for comprehension.

Scholastic Readers are designed to support your child's efforts to learn how to read at every age and every stage. Enjoy helping your child learn to read and love to read.

> —**Francie Alexander**
> Chief Education Officer
> Scholastic Education

Ms. Frizzle

Liz

Written by Jeanette Lane.
Illustrated by Carolyn Bracken.

Based on *The Magic School Bus* books
written by Joanna Cole and illustrated by Bruce Degen.

The author would like to thank Dr. Jim Muzzi
for his expert advice in preparing this manuscript.

ISBN-13: 978-0-439-80107-2
ISBN-10: 0-439-80107-9

12 11 10 9 8 7 6 5 4   8/0 9/0 10/0 11/0

Designed by Rick DeMonico.

Printed in the U.S.A.   First printing, January 2006

The Magic School Bus® and the Missing Tooth

Arnold   Ralphie   Keesha   Phoebe   Carlos   Tim   Wanda   Dorothy Ann

SCHOLASTIC INC.

New York   Toronto   London   Auckland   Sydney
Mexico City   New Delhi   Hong Kong   Buenos Aires

Ms. Frizzle's class is fun.
She wears funny dresses.
She wears funny shoes.

WE GO ON FUNNY TRIPS.

WE GO ON THE MAGIC SCHOOL BUS.

YOU'VE NEVER SEEN
SUCH A FUNNY BUS.

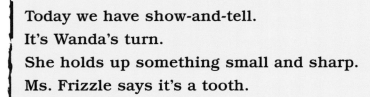

Today we have show-and-tell.
It's Wanda's turn.
She holds up something small and sharp.
Ms. Frizzle says it's a tooth.

We all look closely at the tooth.
We look in our mouths.
That tooth doesn't belong to us!

We are in a classroom.
We wonder why we are here.
Then we see why.
We're flying toward Maria, Carlos's sister!

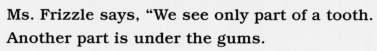

Ms. Frizzle says, "We see only part of a tooth.
Another part is under the gums.
It is called the root.
The root holds a tooth in place.
It is attached to the jawbone."

We look at the shape of the teeth.
Some are flat and some are sharp.
We look at our missing tooth.
It doesn't match.
It is too pointy.

We think our field trip is over,
but we are wrong.
Ms. Frizzle says we are going to a farm.

There are lots of animals on the farm.
We see horses, cows, and sheep.
They are in a field.

ALL THOSE ANIMALS EAT GRASS.

WATCH OUT, MS. FRIZZLE...

...OR ONE WILL EAT US!

Ms. Frizzle must not have heard us.
She is flying the bus right at a horse.
Just then, the horse opens its mouth.
Ms. Frizzle yells, "Yee-hah!"

Now we are in the horse's mouth.
The sharp front teeth cut off big bites of grass.
The back teeth chew up the grass. In between,
there is a space with no teeth at all!

The horse's teeth are *not* pointy.
They are *not* like our missing tooth.
Ms. Frizzle says, "Let's find more teeth!"

Next we see a lazy barn cat.
It is yawning, so we can see its teeth.
The front ones are very sharp!

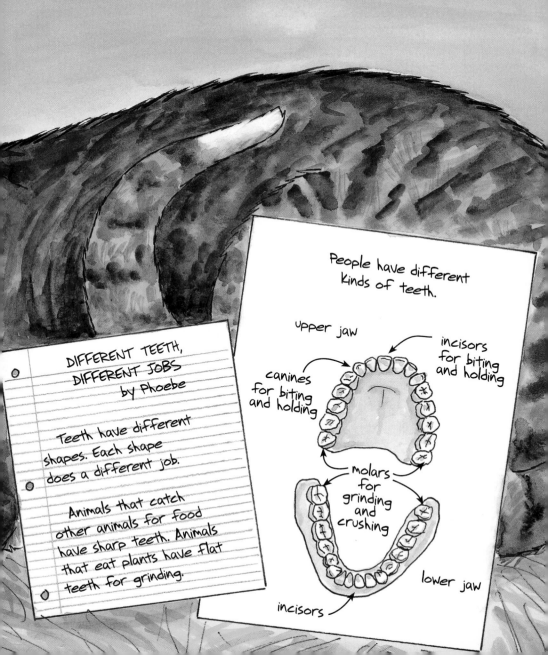

DIFFERENT TEETH,
DIFFERENT JOBS
by Phoebe

Teeth have different
shapes. Each shape
does a different job.

Animals that catch
other animals for food
have sharp teeth. Animals
that eat plants have flat
teeth for grinding.

People have different
kinds of teeth.

upper jaw

incisors
for biting
and holding

canines
for biting
and holding

molars
for
grinding
and
crushing

lower jaw

incisors

The cat's teeth look more like the missing tooth.
But our tooth is smaller than the cat's teeth.
Ms. Frizzle says it is time to go back to school.
We wonder why.

"How did the tooth end up
in our classroom?" Wanda asks.
We all look at one another.
Who lost the tooth?
Just then, our class lizard gives us a smile.

Now the bus is a bus again.
And we know the missing tooth is
a lizard's tooth.
D.A. tells us that lizards like Liz eat
insects, spiders, and other small animals.

Tooth Trivia

Decide which mouth belongs to which animal.
There is a cat, a horse, a human, and a crocodile.
The answers are below.

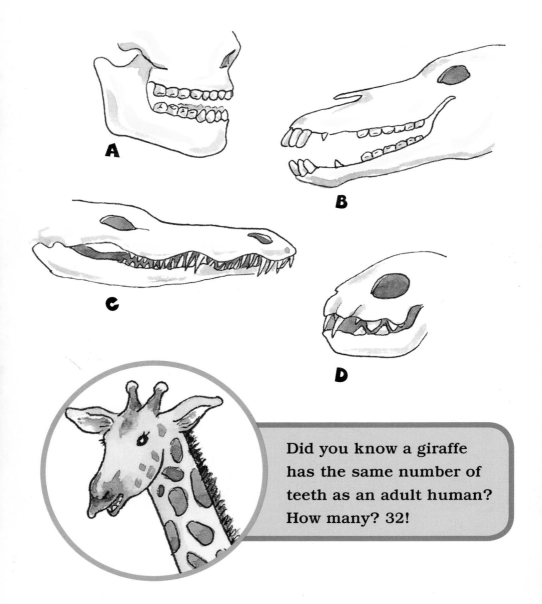

Did you know a giraffe
has the same number of
teeth as an adult human?
How many? 32!

A: human; B: horse; C: crocodile; and D: cat